D0027991

THE ARRANGEMENT

Vol. 15

H.M. Ward

H.M. WARD PRESS

www.SexyAwesomeBooks.com

COPYRIGHT

H.M. WARD PRESS

First Edition: June 2014

ISBN: 9781630350277

CHAPTER 1

I stagger backward and mutter things that make no sense before my hands fly over my mouth. Images flash before my eyes of things I've said to Amber and how Naked Guy tried to hurt me. The memories dance like restless ghosts, conjuring an eruption of emotions. Now they're both dead. Gone. Amber sits there staring blankly with her eyes open. I turn and vomit on the hallway floor. Sean grabs my arm and pulls me away, all the while he's talking to Gabe, who's nodding. The old guy closes the door.

"That was supposed to be me." I swallow hard, not realizing I spoke aloud. My eyes are too wide, and my heart is racing too fast. My legs twitch like I need to run but they won't move.

Sean has a tight grip on my wrist. He tugs, so I look up at him. "Nothing will happen to you." He speaks with such certainty, as if he knows he can protect me, but how can he know that? How can he be sure?

Stomach churning, my eyes cut to him as we race down the stairwell. My voice quivers when I speak, "He knows me. This is personal and it's about me." I don't really think about what I'm saying, it's just a gut impression that's taken hold of my heart. Something about this makes me think it, and the thought won't shake. I feel it in my bones and I just know it's true.

Sean shoves through the metal door, out of the dorm, and into the parking lot. Before I know it, we're in his car and lost in traffic. That's when he speaks. "Why do you think he knows you?"

My eyes fixate on nothing and scan every car, every tree, and every person as the car crawls through the gridlock. "It looked angry, not random. Amber saw him, but the guy under the bedding didn't. Those shots, the places where he put the bullets." I stop speaking and cringe. The shots to the groin and shoulders didn't kill him. The murderer made him suffer before putting the final bullet in his body. "It just didn't seem impersonal to me. If that was you…"

I suck in a shaky breath and bite my tongue. I couldn't bare it. We were supposed to be in that room, the dead couple should have been us. Amber wasn't supposed to be there. But, that means this isn't some insane vigilante doing a moral cleansing of Black's hookers, not if it left two of my acquaintances dead. "What did I do? I don't even know what I did to deserve this? Sean?" I'm panicking, pleading, looking over at him.

Sean swallows hard and those big blue eyes are filled with fear. He's going to lose me. Either I'm going to walk out or someone is going to put a bullet in my head. I ramble about the mistaken identity of the call girl in the hotel room, how everyone thought it was one of Black's girls. The whole thing seems like a scattered mess, but it's not. I just don't see the common thread. There has to be one. I have to find it before he makes another attempt, before more people die.

Numbly, I tell him, "Take me to Henry Thomas."

Sean glances over at me like I'm crazy. "No." His voice is firm and sounds more like a scold than a response. There's no way he'll let me near Henry, but he's the only common thread I see.

I explain my thoughts to Sean. "He's the only connection. We have to confront him. We can't wait for him to come for me. Go there, now."

Sean shakes his head. "Avery, you're not thinking."

"Sean, I can't take this anymore!" My hands are balled and slam into my lap. They're clenched so tightly that my nails bite into the soft flesh of my palms.

Suddenly, Sean slams down the accelerator pedal and I'm thrown back into my seat. He cuts across traffic like a racecar driver, and gets off the parkway before turning around. We were headed toward the strip club, but now we aren't. I glance over at him. "Where are we going?"

His features are stoic and the mask is in place, the one that I tried so hard to shatter so the real Sean would shine through. He grips the wheel tightly, making his knuckles pale. "I need to speak with someone."

"Who? Everyone is at the club."

"No, not everyone." He works his jaw and takes a moment to reveal the rest of his thoughts to me. He darts through traffic, cutting in and out with ease. He knows this car and how to handle her as well as he knows every inch of my body. When he glances over at me, he adds, "The most sly, cunning person is at the mansion. I need to speak with my mother."

CHAPTER 2

When we walk inside the Ferro residence, it's quiet. Sean paces the grand foyer like a schoolboy with a bad grade. He taps his fingers to his palms over and over again, while he waits for his mother to accept his arrival. I can't imagine it. How is this a home? How is Constance a mother if she makes her son wait at the door—but those were the directions. No one is to be admitted into the residence this afternoon without her permission.

A butler returns with a grave expression on his face, and bows to Sean. "Mrs. Ferro states that you may wait for her in her favorite room." The man turns and starts to walk away. We follow him down opulent hallways and past shiny marble statues. Priceless paintings line the walls from various artists that haven't walked the earth for ages.

I point at one, gaping, "Is that real?" I recognize it from a textbook. The colors are a medley of blues and a man stands with his back to us, staring out at the sea that crashes around him. I remember the piece because I liked the way it made me feel when I looked at it. I didn't know if the man was happy, sad, or waiting for someone to return. The way he stares at the sea is the way I stare at the stars, wondering and waiting for something to save me from this hellish life I've fallen into. At the same time, his posture, the squareness of his shoulders, and the way he clasps his hands behind his back state that he is not a victim in the least. His confidence, despite the sea spray and the rocks that symbolize peril, is inspiring. I stop in front of it unable to look away.

Sean gives me a small smile and takes my pointing finger in his hand to turn me toward him before he nods. "It is. But, you must never discuss money with my mother.

Ever. That includes her treasures, as she calls them." He tips his head toward the painting.

"Why did we come here?" I ask, just as we round the corner to a glass room filled with flowers and plants. In the center of the room is a clearing with a beautiful antique white table with two chairs. A bottle of wine sits on top, opened. Constance Ferro is standing in the center, wearing a silk robe and a pair of matching slippers with a glass of wine in her hand. She swirls the contents carefully, examining it as if it might be poisoned.

"Yes, my thoughts exactly." Constance is wearing a blood-colored duster with a floral pattern burnt into the silk. It makes her hair look like spun gold. After placing the wine glass down, she clasps her hands together and then parts them as she tips her head to the side with a viper-like smile on her aged lips. "What on earth would make my most resentful offspring dare to show his face unannounced?"

Sean's gaze flicks over his mother's outfit without concealing his disdain. "Another consort?"

"No, a lover. Consort is such a cold word, Sean. Really. I don't know where you get it from. Either way, you're wasting my time and I'm needed elsewhere. You mustn't spoil other people's delights." She smiles so falsely that I think her porcelain face might crack. "So tell me the reason for your joyous visit, or keep your silent thoughts to yourself, turn, and walk away." Constance continues her serene pose the entire time she speaks, like her words aren't barbed and filled with venom.

Sean stiffens. I can't imagine what's going through his mind. I glance over at her and then back at him. If I didn't know better, I'd think Sean is afraid of her. That makes two things that scare the bejesus out of him—love and his mother. No wonder he's so messed up.

When Sean doesn't speak, Constance makes an annoyed sound, and turns on her heel to walk away. I blurt out, "There was blood." My throat is still too tight to speak, but it's enough. She stops and turns slowly, looking back at me.

Constance crosses the room, one slippered foot at a time, and looks down into my face. A dark brow raises high and disappears under her hair. My heart thumps in my chest and feels like I've tripped down a staircase.

"Where?" She glares at me when she spits out the word.

I maintain eye contact even though it's like staring down a rabid bear. There's no doubt in my mind that this woman could eat me alive. I steady my voice as best I can. "In my room. In his room. Everywhere."

Sean is still silent. His jaw is mashed shut and his fingers clenched. His mother looks over at him. "And you think it's *him*?" It sounds like she's referring to someone that Sean already knows.

"It's possible." Sean's terse tone doesn't go unnoticed.

Constance laughs. "It can't be—he's not even in New York."

Sean's arms fold over his chest and he exhales loudly. He demands, "Who's seen him?"

I raise a finger. Interjecting, "Who are we talking about?" But they ignore me.

Constance mirrors her son's stance. "Everyone. Dear God, Sean. You surely don't think he'd do something like this?"

Sean becomes the man I first met, intimidating and overbearing. He seems to grow an inch or two in that moment. His deep voice resonates as he steps closer to his mother with determination in his voice. "Actually, I do, otherwise I wouldn't be standing here. You were friends with his family. You know where his father is, and I'm guessing he's waiting for you now." They glare at each other in a silent storm. There's so much passing between them, so much that I don't know.

Sean finally breaks the quiet standoff. "Where is his son?"

Constance laughs and her features change, softening quickly. "His son had his ribs broken because of your toy here, and wants to avoid you at the moment. Don't worry, I'm sure he'll come after you again, just not right now."

I blurt out, "Are you talking about Henry?" They both look at me.

Constance sneers and then addresses Sean. "Take a long moment to stop and consider who the real target is here. A dead pilot, dead call girls, all who were supposed to be near you, my dear."

"Then, why did he keep returning to Avery's room?" Sean asks.

"Because you were there." Constance appears smug and turns away, as if she's had enough and is going to leave.

"How do you know all of this?" I ask, and she looks amused. The pilot? How does she know about him? Does she know I killed him or just that he's missing? Maybe she's bluffing and doesn't know anything, but from the look on Sean's face, that can't be true.

His mother turns toward me with a narrowed gaze. "Avery Stanz, it's my job to know everything from the color of your eyes to the amount of money you have in your checking account. You're fucking my son. Enjoy his body all you want, but you won't get a dime of my fortune."

My hackles rise. I step forward to chew her out, but Sean places a hand on my shoulder. He speaks over me. "She doesn't want to be a part of this family, Mother. I already asked her. Do you see a ring? No, so there's your answer, and you can stop behaving so defensively." He doesn't look at me or let me speak. Instead, he steps closer to his mother, leaving me behind them. In a low voice he demands, "Find out what I need to know."

"You mean, find out if it was Henry Thomas?" Constance is practically laughing at him.

Through his teeth, Sean hisses, "Yes."

"And what favor will you grant in return?" Constance tips her head to the side and swings the tassel on her gown once before slapping it into the center of her palm. She does it without looking, and with such ease that I get the distinct impression that she's whipped people and thoroughly enjoys it. I wonder if she laid a strap to Sean, if some of the mental scars are from physical abuse. She seems like the Mommy Dearest type, except her lash isn't given in a fit of rage—it's cold and calculated.

My jaw drops at her vile comment. I can't help it and speak out of shock. "You think that someone is trying to kill your son and it's a favor to help keep him alive?"

"It is a favor." She snaps at me, before giving me a stare so evil that the Devil must have taught it to her. Her gaze flicks back to her son. "So, what will it be, Sean? Ditching the trailer trash and going home sounds like an amiable bargain. I hear your wife-to-be is missing you."

Sean watches his mother for a second and I'm horrified because she's talking about me. She thinks I don't know about his fiancée, but I already do. Nothing in the world would make Sean agree to that bargain, but he puts his hand out and she takes it.

Sean replies stoically, "Done."

Constance grins triumphantly as they shake hands. "Wonderful."

CHAPTER 3

I'm not wearing Sean's ring. I have no right to blow up at him and scream in his face, but I want to. The ride back to the club is filled with tense silence. Sean grips the wheel until I think it's going to break off in his hands. His forehead is drawn together forming angry lines, and I know he's lost in thought, livid.

I stare out my window, equally enraged. He accepted help from the devil and traded me in like I was worthless. I was his bargaining chip. He threw me away like a piece of trash. Sean didn't even hesitate. It feels like he ripped my heart from my chest and handed it to his mother. I can't take this anymore.

When he pulls into the club's parking lot, Sean slams on the breaks and jumps out. He doesn't open my door, or wait for me. He disappears into the building without a word. I trail after him, not knowing what to do or say. I'm furious, but I can't react, not now. Not here.

When I push through the door, no one is around. I hear Sean's voice behind the closed office door. He's arguing with Jon, and it sounds like Bryan is in there too because someone is laughing. Only he'd be crazy enough to laugh at Sean when rage is pouring off the man in sheets.

There's a worn black couch in the back corner. I head over and sit down hard, slipping lower into the seat until I look like a sulking teenager. Leaning my head against the backrest, I stare at the ceiling. There are two ways to look at this situation—I rejected Sean, so he's agreed to his mother's request because it doesn't change anything. Or, he's trying to protect me and is willing to give me up to do it.

A tear is about to fall from the corner of my eye when the seat next to me dips. "Hey," Trystan says, and hands me a tissue.

I have no idea why Sean hates him so much. Trystan is one of the nicest guys I know. I take it and dab. "Thanks."

He doesn't ask me what's wrong, or pry. He just sits there, slumped back like me, and crosses his arms over his chest. That ring glints from below his shirt as he stares at nothing. "So, I'm thinking philosophy is bullshit. The more I think about it, the more it seems like fate is a bunch of crap. I mean, that's the same thing as walking around and letting luck guide your life, right?"

This guy always surprises me. There's a sharp mind behind the rocker façade. I wonder how many people know how intelligent he is, how he's always thinking. "Maybe, but I wouldn't know because I only seem to have bad luck. Dead parents, no house, shitty boss, crazy ex-boyfriend…" My voice trails off as I stare at the office door.

Trystan doesn't look. He sighs deeply and slips his hand over mine. It's a gesture meant to comfort. "I could say the same thing. My mother ran away, it was my fault, my dad beat the shit out of me, half the time I slept outside, and I'm totally alone. The thing I want most, I don't have and I never will." He shrugs as though he's accepted it.

I glance at the office door, wishing for a version of Sean that is more mirage than real. "Same here."

"Yeah, but I was an asshole and let it happen. You have a choice. The guy that has your heart is in the same building. He hasn't left you." Trystan looks over at me and then at his hand. He goes to pull it away, but I stop him and look at his hand. The tips of his fingers are calloused from playing his guitar.

I run my fingers over the hardened pads and ask, "So what's stopping you? Fate? I thought that was bullshit. Call her."

Trystan offers a crooked grin as his gaze falls to the floor. He seems so much younger than Sean, more innocent, but equally battered. He still wears his heart on his sleeve occasionally and I can see it now, shattered into a million pieces. "It's not that simple." His voice has a lost sound and I know his mind is a million miles away, remembering something—someone.

"It never is." I lean into him and we tip our heads together. "We seem the same, sometimes."

"I noticed," I feel him smile softly and then he looks down at me. Trystan moves slowly and tucks a piece of hair behind my ear. Watching me closely, he speaks so softly, so sincerely, that his voice feels like a caress, "Some people think that each soul was torn in two and that you'll know when you find it, that true happiness can only be found when the two souls are reunited." His blue gaze flicks between my eyes, but I know he isn't talking about me.

"Do you believe that?"

"I did, once."

"And now?" My voice is nearly a whisper. Trystan is way too close and somehow both his hands have made their way to my cheeks. His touch is so gentle, so careful, as he wipes away tears that I didn't feel rolling down my face.

"Now?" He smiles for a second and then it fades. "I'm willing to admit that I don't know anything, not anymore. Sometimes life takes a wrong turn and it goes unnoticed 'til a certain point. Now, I wonder, and I can't help it." He leans in and presses his lips to mine. The action catches me off guard, but I don't slap him or pull away. Trystan feels like an old blanket, warm and familiar. The small touch means so much and nothing at all. It's almost as if it were a test, as if he wanted to see if my lips felt like hers—like the woman he's lost.

Trystan doesn't taste like Sean or hold me the same way. He's gentle, seeking, asking if he should be there, waiting for me rather than forcing himself on me. It's different and I can't help but wonder if Sean's kisses were like these years ago before Amanda shattered his soul.

It's so unexpected and so gentle. I need comfort. I'm scared to death and haven't had someone to hug, or hold me tight. Sometimes those silent gestures mean the most. They're the glue that holds our fragile lives together.

My lips linger, tingling from the contact. It's at that moment that Sean speaks. "Wow, you didn't even wait until the bed was cold. Or did he hire you from Black?"

CHAPTER 4

Trystan pulls his face back, but holds onto me, breathing in slowly before he stands. I want to fight with Sean, but Trystan is between us. He's too calm, too unintimidated, which makes Sean irate. Trystan runs his fingers through his long hair, pushing it out of his eyes. "If you treated her just a little bit better, just a little bit kinder, she'd still be yours. You're too blind to see what she is if you think she's just a call girl."

I was ready to scream at Sean, but the way Trystan speaks deflates me, as it does Sean. Sean's still mad, prickled like a cactus, but he doesn't speak. He allows Trystan to walk away, leaving the two of us staring at one another. That kiss was nothing like Sean's. I could feel Trystan's anguish, the need to forget, to be lost in someone else. He's mourning, deeply.

So is Sean, but his grief comes across differently, and if he's not in control he feels weak. It's a result of losing Amanda, I know it is, but sometimes I crave that soft touch. I glance at Trystan for a second, watching him tuck his hands into his pockets and disappear around the corner. His shoulders are hunched and his head is hung. He looks nothing like the arrogant singer that struts around on stage.

"You like him." Sean speaks and brings my gaze back to his.

I'm silent for a moment and then say, "Does it matter? I'm not asking to be mean, but does it honestly matter? You promised your mother that you're through with me."

"You're not wearing my ring, so there's nothing more to talk about." Sean ends the conversation and I feel the hole in my chest heaving with a weight that I cannot bear.

So I just nod, and tuck my chin so he can't see my eyes, and let my hair fall forward. I don't tuck it behind my ear this time, I let it dangle and shield me. I steady my voice even though I want to cry. "So, what now?"

"Now we hide you until we find out where Henry Thomas has been."

"Sean, I'm tired of hiding." I'm tired of hiding, of fighting, of trying to love someone who doesn't want to be loved. I'm so weary that I feel my seams are coming undone and I can't hold it together any longer. There's blood on my hands—I killed someone. The guilt from that lingers, never truly leaving me even though I had to do it. Rationality doesn't erase guilt or the worry that someone will find his body.

Sean crouches in front of me, lowering his toned body until he's in my face, and speaks so softly that it scares me. Between his tone and the look in his eye, I know he's desperate. This person, the murderer, is a step ahead of him and he can't stand it. His nose just barely brushes mine. His lips curl as he articulates each sound, so that I know there's no room for debate. "Your roommate had a bullet in her brain. I will not let that happen to you. You don't have a choice in the matter. We're hiding you until this situation is resolved and I know you're not in danger."

Sean stands and yells, "Scott!" He calls out once, then again. Trystan emerges from the back of the building, standing in the shadows of the dark hallway. "Take her away from here and hide her until I can resolve a few things." The two men stare at each other. There's an understanding between them that I can't fathom. Sean hates Trystan, why is he handing me off to him?

Before I can speak, Trystan nods. "Done."

They glare at each other for a long moment, then Sean adds, "And Scott, if I can find her, you're a dead man."

CHAPTER 5

When did I lose control over my life? I'm a college dropout and that's the least of my problems. My dreams shattered one by one, like glass balls falling from a dead Christmas tree. I made one bad decision after another and I can't stand it anymore.

Trystan's been quiet since the confrontation with Sean. I have no idea what's going through his mind. One moment he's spewing philosophy and the next he's looking at me like I'm a mirage. I don't know if he's attracted to me. That kiss is messing with my mind. Is that what it'd be like? Are normal guys doting and sweet? Trystan hasn't demanded a thing from me.

He's nothing like Sean, but one thing is the same. I don't think he sees it, but I do.

Broken hearts don't mend.

We're in Trystan's apartment, well, a condo, I guess. It's the hellhole where he grew up. The place is worn and hasn't been lived in for years. A thick layer of dust covers every inch, every surface. A ratty couch and chair are in the small living room, set in front of an old TV that probably doesn't work. It's the fat kind that looks more like a piece of furniture than electronics.

Trystan pulls open a drawer and tosses me a towel. "I don't come here anymore."

"I can imagine why." I say the comment without giving it much thought. Mistake.

He turns and glares at me. "No, you can't." His azure gaze goes back to wiping down the dining table and chairs, before he hurls the cloth at the wall and sits down hard. Sucking in air, he leans forward and plants his elbows on the table, grabbing fists full of hair. "I shouldn't have come back here."

I stand there like an idiot, not knowing what to do. This place is like poison to him.

I can see it soaking into his veins and choking him to death. He's withering before my eyes. I pad toward him and place a hand on his shoulder. "Trystan, I'm sorry. I'm sorry to put you through this. I'm sorry you're here. I'm sorry you crossed my path and I sucked you into this." My jaw hangs open, but the only sound that pours out is silent regret.

After a moment, my hand slips away and his breathing slows. Still looking down, he tells me, "The last time I was here my old man tried to kill me. Then they found out who I was. It was like a line of dominos. One fell right after the other, good and bad, stirring together until I was so turned around that I didn't know what to do. I had people then, people who helped me. You have no one, except Sean, and in case you didn't notice, the Ferro's are like acid." Trystan sits up and turns. His face is blank, eerily expressionless.

"But Jon's your best friend. So is Bryan." Shaking my head, I ask, "I don't get it. Then, why are you always with them?"

He smiles like he's the stupidest man alive. It's the humble grin of a man that realizes his own naiveté. Sighing deeply, he runs a hand through his hair and looks up at me. "The same reason you're with Sean. I thought they were a little battered—hell, who's not—but they're not like that. Are they?"

When I don't answer, he stands and walks along the tiny kitchen, trailing his finger in the dust. "From the moment I met Jon, I saw what they did to him, the way his family dug in their fangs and sucked him dry. The way they use each other, like they aren't even people, as if they don't matter. Every bite is venomous; every breath taken in that house is poison. They both know it, but there's no way out. I stick around and pick up the pieces, and they do the same for me. Once in a while, I flame out. They can hide things, make it so it never happened, so she never sees." His gaze cuts over to me, before lowering to his dusty finger.

Wiping it on his jeans, he smiles that fake grin of his and tips his head to the side. "Like I said, they're acid—every single one of them. They can clean up a mess so that there are no marks left at all, but they poison everything they touch."

I defend him before I have time to even think. "Sean's not like that."

"Oh?" Trystan folds his arms over his chest. "Elaborate. Enlighten me, Call Girl. Tell me how he's kind and compassionate, about how he takes care of you and puts you first. Tell me about the height of the pedestal he's placed you on, and that you worry about falling off...that he thinks too highly of you. That you're just a girl, but this man thinks you're more stunning than a star hung in the heavens." As he speaks, he steps toward me, one slow step at a time. My heart races as he talks and strings those words together so effortlessly, describing a vivid scene from a life that I don't know. My spine straightens and it's as if I'm being slapped, but he doesn't stop, not until we're nose to nose. "Say it, Call Girl. Tell me."

His breath mingles with mine. I can barely speak without our lips brushing together, but I don't step back. "Just because he's not like that doesn't mean he doesn't care."

Trystan's eyes narrow to slits and his tongue becomes sharp. "Oh, I know. He cares about controlling you, using you, and what else am I forgetting? Oh yeah, claiming you. You're an object to him, something to be won." He lifts a lock of my hair and then drops it as if I wasn't a prize worth fighting for.

I puff up, snapping, "You don't know him the way I do. He's not like that. A broken heart manifests differently in different people. Don't pretend to know how he feels or what he thinks."

Trystan smiles sadly. "That man has no heart. Maybe he did once, but it's gone now."

"How do you know?" I shove a finger into his chest and scold him. "How can you tell me, so definitively, that Sean's a heartless monster?" This entire conversation is touching a nerve that runs deep. It scares me beyond comprehension, because sometimes I see it in Sean's eyes-- that he's fallen too far—and he's out of reach.

I'd once thought love could save anyone, but I'm not so certain now. The box, what he did to me, the way he seemed to come back to life, as if he were repressing something dark within him that fights for freedom—is that all that's left of Sean Ferro?

And this man, this rock star, thinks he knows without a doubt. I make a face. He doesn't know Sean better than I do—no one does.

But, Trystan doesn't react the way I expect. Instead, he gently wraps his fingers around mine and pushes my hand away. The corner of his mouth tips up in a look that's pure and somber. Looking me straight in the eye, he whispers, "Because we're the same man." The way he says it sends a chill down my spine. This smiling, carefree guy is not the same as Sean. How can he say that?

It's as if Trystan can read my mind. His dark lashes lower, as does his voice, "Give it a few years and you'll see. The difference between us is wire-thin and time is the enemy. His wife died and he blamed himself, he always has, no matter what the papers say. I suffered heartache that was caused by my own hand as well. The aftermath wasn't as gruesome, but the soul can't tell. It just knows she's gone and it's my fault. My heart dies within me, day-by-day, beat-by-beat. I hide it with a smile and wiseass comments, but my pain and suffering is mine and nothing will free me from it. I'm in a cage and there is no key. Sean's been imprisoned for too long. Nothing will set him free. No—not even you."

Trystan's words slice through me like a blade. The air is pulled from my lungs and my response is instant. I slap him across the face and am shocked to feel the sting of his skin against my palm. Sean would have stopped me. Trystan let me strike him. He doesn't grab my wrist or try to force me to do anything.

Instead, the man smiles one of those delicious grins he's known for. "Keep fighting, Avery. That's the only way to know you're still alive."

Shock rolls down my back, making my hackles raise higher. "You think I'm caged too? You think I'm going to be like him? Like you? You're nothing like him! He doesn't talk to you. Why should I believe a thing you say?"

"Because like calls to like and soul calls to soul. Pain that etches us to the bone leaves a mark and I see it on him, just as I see it on you. We're all the same, Call Girl. There's no escape, not for us." Trystan's words are like poems and they roll off his tongue as easily as a drop of rain falls from the sky.

"How can you live like that? Day in and day out?" I gape at him, with my brows pinched together and my heart beating hard. The man has a hole in his heart the size of his head, but he still spouts poetry that's rich with beauty and an understanding of the world that I severely lack.

Trystan laughs bitterly and runs his fingers through his hair. "I don't know. It's the remnants of a dying soul, I guess. The embers always burn brightest just before they go out." He sighs, and suddenly realizes he's been holding the ring that hangs around his neck. He drops it like it's hot iron, and swallows hard. "I better find some blankets. We can't turn anything on. The press is always watching for me and if this place suddenly lights up, they'll find me. And if they find me, they'll find you."

CHAPTER 6

Trystan hid some bedding and money here a few years back. He explains briefly, but doesn't tell me why. "They've been in plastic, so they have that weird scent, but it's better than sleeping on the couch. Here." He tosses me a bed in a bag, complete with pillows. He opens another one for himself and lays it on the center of the floor before plopping down in the center and kicking off his shoes. His eyes fixate on a rust-colored stain on the wall. I can't imagine the demons that must be pressing in on him from being here.

Trystan seems to like talking about philosophy, so I try. Admittedly, I suck at it. I don't have the same aptitude for it that he does. There's something about him, and the way he looks at the world, that's rare.

I lay on top of my blankets after spreading them out next to his. I lie in the dark, on my back, and tuck my hands under the pillow so they're over my head and stretch. The day's events are catching up with me and I can't bear to think about them. My gaze flicks to my shoes, which are next to me on the floor. Trystan's wearing his jeans, and strips off his shirt. The ring remains at the center of his chest, right above his heart. He never takes it off. My eyes slip over him. He's a few years younger than Sean, leaner, with hard muscles beneath paler skin. There's not a tattoo on him, which is weird because I would have sworn I'd seen photo-shoots with him covered in them.

"So, have you always been drawn to philosophy or is that a new thing?"

Trystan's attention had been elsewhere, lost in the past. His hands are tucked behind his neck and he's lying flat on his back. He blinks before his gaze cuts to the side. "People don't change."

"Ah, so I'll take that as a yes. And the ring? Is that part of how people don't change?" I know I shouldn't ask about it, but I do. There's no way that hairy cat is going back in the bag.

Trystan doesn't answer. He stares at the ceiling, silent. I watch his chest rise and fall. Rolling over, I curl onto my side. I don't know how he can lay like that. Every breath I take feels like a knife in my chest, digging in deeper and deeper. I lower my gaze. "I'm sorry. I shouldn't have asked."

Trystan's blue gaze wanders over to mine. "Let's try something different. Instead of looking behind us, let's look ahead. We're both stuck in the past. Tell me, what do you want, Call Girl? I assume this isn't the life you would have chosen."

He hasn't confided anything in me, so my answer is childish. "Why should I tell you anything?"

"Confession is good for the soul, and since yours and mine are both ailing, it seemed like a good idea. If it's too much for you, I understand. The future unnerves some people, because they have to free themselves from their past to get there."

"There's a little bit of a dichotomy going on in that brain of yours. You said there was no freedom from past actions." I waggle my eyebrows at him and smile. I understand something, and I've caught a flaw in his perfect thoughts. Score!

He smiles for a split second. "So, you were listening."

I roll onto my back and look at the yellowed ceiling. "I'm always listening. I have no idea what I'm doing half the time, but it's not from tuning everyone out."

"You're too hard on yourself."

Silence surrounds us for a long time, and then I finally say what I've thought all along. "You hardly ever say my name." He glances over at me but doesn't reply. "I remind you of her, don't I?" I remind you of the woman you lost, the one you're still in love with.

Trystan inhales deeply and rolls onto his side, facing me. "It's easier to not call you by your name. Saying a profession conjures you alone. Reaching for a name is dangerous, especially when the woman a guy is with reminds him of another." He watches me, gauging my reaction.

"What do you think will happen if you say her name by accident? Do you think I'll be offended? Or spontaneously combust? Poof." I make a fist and open it as I say the last word, before smiling at him and then shoving his shoulder when he doesn't answer. "It won't bother me."

"Ah, but it will bother me. So, it's safer this way." His smile is so sad, so tragic.

"But it keeps you trapped. You're with her, but she's not with you."

"I could say the same thing about you and Sean. You gave him your heart and he still has it, yet you're here with me." I look away. Too many painful memories blur together and I can't bear to watch them flash behind my eyes. Trystan reaches for me, taking my hand in his, and tangling our fingers together. He repeats, "The future—what do you want? Something real, not a fantasy."

He means not Sean with a picket fence and a smile on his face. After a moment, I try to picture something, anything. I finally confess, "I don't know. Everything got messed up."

I don't know what changed in that moment, but suddenly I'm telling him how my parents died, then about college, how I was worried about getting into graduate school, but I never even made it to graduation. Guilt bubbles up about Amber and Naked Guy, even though he hurt me. They both did, but it's my fault they're dead. Their lives are over, and no matter how nasty they were, the guilt is eating me alive.

Trystan takes my chin and holds my gaze. "All those things are behind you. What's ahead of you? Where do you want to go from here?" His blue eyes are a shade darker than Sean's, with flecks of amber scattered like golden coins tossed into the sea.

When he releases me, I confess, "That's just it. There is nowhere to go. I have no money, Miss Black won't let me leave, and I'm not stupid. I know she doesn't want me on Long Island to be a madam. She's lining things up so it'll look like I was the one in charge if things go to Hell and not her. She'll be protected behind her wall of thugs and filing cabinets. I'm barely a call girl, never mind a madam."

"How many men, or uh—women—have you slept with?" He almost blushes asking the question. The way his gaze drops is so sweet and unlike anything I've ever seen him do.

I bump his shoulder. "I told you, I'm the worst call girl there ever was—I had one client, who I only slept with after falling in love with him, and the other clients didn't get sex." I laugh because it seems too ridiculous to be real.

He looks at me like it can't be true. "Are you serious? You've only been with Sean?"

I shrug. "It's not like I felt like dating after my parents died, and I didn't want to get knocked up. It would have made life impossible." My goofy smile fades and I roll onto my back, away from him, rubbing the chill off my arms. "I pushed away every guy who tried to get to know me. Well, except Marty, but he was gay."

"Was?"

"Don't get me started on that. My eye will twitch and I'll go all bitch-o on you, and I'd rather not. Remember? We're looking ahead. So, what's in your future, Rock Star?" I glance over at him and wonder what secrets he'll reveal.

Trystan is too quiet, and when I glance his way I notice how he's looking at me. I like it and I don't. Conflict rears within me, because he seems great, but – Sean.

You left Sean and Sean left you. That's over.

Trystan slides next to me and pushes up on his elbow. Looking down at me, he says, "I don't know. You tell me."

"Trystan…" I want to say no, but I can't. I want the embrace he's about to offer. I want the comfort that Sean's never given. "You're not over her."

"And you're not over him." He doesn't move. "Tell me you're not curious, that you haven't wondered about it, about me."

Through my lashes, I look up at him and tell him the truth. "Every girl alive wonders about you."

"So, one night and nothing more. A kiss to comfort, an embrace to heal a weeping heart—I'm not him—you're not her. We both know that, but we don't have to be alone." Trystan is leaning over me, his body only brushing mine when he breathes. He doesn't move. He remains poised above me, looking down. He smiles once and then it fades. "If you want me, for anything, I'm right next to you." He kisses my lips lightly, once, before he returns to his blankets.

I don't know what to do. I love Sean. I want Sean, but he's gone. I told him I couldn't do it anymore and gave him back his ring. Then he said to his mother that we were nothing, and that he was leaving. Sean's gone. That part of my life is over and thinking about it makes me want to cry, balling into my pillows.

But Trystan's words ring in my ears. *Look forward.* Would a night in his arms be so bad? I want to be held and told that everything will work out. I want to feel loved, and right now I don't, but there's a cure less than two feet away. I could reach out and touch his shoulder. That's all it would take.

What do I want? It's a simple question, but I don't know the answer. Actually, I know what I want, but it doesn't exist. I want Sean. I want his arms around me and I want him to do everything in his power to keep me. Instead, he handed me off and made a trade with his mother. I was gone before our bed was cold. The thought weighs heavily on my heart.

People don't change. I once thought I wanted the monster within, but it's much darker and more dominant than I thought possible. I can't handle it—I can't handle Sean—and I can't be with someone who frightens me. I don't want to be with anyone anymore, but Trystan's offer lingers in the back of my mind.

People do things like he suggested, a night together, to offer comfort and companionship. I like him, I do, but I'm not over Sean. Trystan is clearly stuck on someone else. It seems foolish to be with someone when it's not the one you want. But what do I know?

CHAPTER 7

Closing my eyes, I roll over and try to find sleep. But the water comes, and the nightmares turn real. Somewhere between wake and sleep I can't stand it any longer. I jut upright and scream, waking the man next to me. The windows glow pale yellow from the streetlight and I remember where I am. I can't breathe.

"Avery?" Trystan's voice is soft, and his hand gently touches my shoulder. "Are you all right?"

I shake my head, unable to speak. "I have a cure for that. Hold on." He's up, disappears, and comes back with a couple of bottles and plastic cups. "Drink up."

"What is it?"

"Something that will make you forget the pain," he looks into the cup, "for a little while anyway."

"What makes you think—"?

He cuts me off. "I don't think, I know. When life punches you and you can't punch back, this is what happens. Deal with it tomorrow. For now, drink up." He pours the same mixture into his own cup and clinks it to mine before taking a swig of the contents.

I do the same and nearly spew. "Holy shitty fat cow!" My jaw hangs open as I try to get the taste out of my mouth. "What the hell is this?"

"Knockout juice. Pray the house doesn't catch fire." He takes another swig and blinks as if he can't focus.

I already feel it. My stomach is empty and this tastes like a funky mixture of hard liquor. My head feels strange, but I take another sip and can't help making faces. "This stuff tastes like tar mixed with gasoline."

"Avery, dear, stop drinking tar." He finally smiles sincerely and I see his shoulders lose some of their slump. The tension that was held deep within him begins to fade as we sit and talk about nothing.

Finally, I say, "You weren't asleep, were you?"

Staring into the bottom of an empty cup, he sighs and tosses it aside. "What makes you say that?"

"You were sitting up before I opened my eyes. I remember." I go to tap my temple and poke myself in the eye. I blink once, shocked that I missed. "I don't drink much."

"No kidding." He laughs, and then adds more seriously, "Yeah, I was up. This place is Hell. There's no peace here." He looks around like he can actually see demons crawling the walls. "That's where he smashed my head into the wall, and over there, that's where he—"

Shivering, I reach over and my fingers touch his bare skin. Trystan stops speaking and looks over at me. I feel so lost, like I'm in a freefall that will never end. I can't stand it. I need someone to hold me and whisper words of comfort in my ear. Something inside me stirs from the intensity of his gaze. When Trystan places his hand over mine he doesn't speak and neither do I.

Maybe it's the drink or maybe it's me, I can't tell, but I don't want him to let go. I want his soft, tender touches. I want him to be Sean. I want so many things that they float through my mind in a myriad of flutters, as gently as a butterfly's wing. I'm drawn to him, to those lips, and that mouth. Trystan never pretends, but this is make-believe. This can't happen. We're both in love with someone else, but he doesn't let go and I don't move away.

Slowly, Trystan slides his palm up my arm to my shoulder. He tips his head to the side and says, "Come here." When his arms wrap around me, I tuck my head under his chin—the way I've wanted to with Sean so many times. As I'm held to his chest, I can hear Trystan's heart is beating hard. His skin is so warm and perfect. I stay, tracing the muscles of his bare arms down to his wrists.

Trystan assumes nothing. He steals no kisses and his hands don't roam. He's a good man and I wish I could mend his heart, but the most I can offer is a brief reprieve.

I feel the cold chain against my arm, and pull away slightly to look down at it. I lift the object and turn it over in my fingers. He watches me, saying nothing. When I put it down, the ring falls into place against his chest. Trystan presses his eyes closed and wraps his fingers around the ring. "Here I've been telling you to let go of the past, but I wear mine around my neck." He yanks at the chain and tosses it to the floor.

Worry rushes through me. I know how hard that must have been. I want to ease his pain and forget mine—just for a moment. It's an innocent thought at first, something meant to be soft and caring. Before Trystan can speak, my lips find his, but things are different this time.

CHAPTER 8

We aren't on a couch and I'm not sober. The world is tipping sideways and it feels like I'm about to fall off the edge and be devoured by monsters. Trystan is my anchor so I cling to him, holding on tight like I'll die if I let go. He does the same and that soft kiss, that simple sweeping of lips changes.

Trystan's hands find my cheeks and he traces the lines of my face, learning the curves of my mouth as he does it. His kisses are tender, though he holds me firmly. I know I'm desired and there's no question that I'm his in that moment, but he doesn't hurt me. There's no pain, not with him, it vanishes and I feel steady for the first time in months.

The way Trystan touches me, the way he tastes me—every aspect is unique to him. The way his tongue strokes my lips and tangles with mine is all his own, the tender touch of his hands on my skin, and the way his thumb pulls my lower lip out ever so slightly so he can suck it into his mouth. My stomach twists as I forget myself. The pain and worries recede as I let him slide his hands over my curves, leading him with my own. The kisses grow hotter and more demanding, more breathless until they aren't enough.

My shirt disappears and I shut my eyes. He lets me move how I want, touch where I want, and take what I want. We forget for a while, and the world that pains us washes away, lost in a drunken lust. I'm not bound or told to face away. He lets me roll him onto his back and cover his chest in kisses before I straddle him. He unbuttons my jeans and slips his hands under the waistband as our hips rock slowly. No one speaks. I hear him sigh or maybe that's me, I'm not certain anymore. Then he digs his fingers into my back, guiding me—showing me what he likes—where he wants to be kissed.

For a moment, I'm lost and I've forgotten, until her name slips from his lips in a whisper almost too quiet to hear. I don't think he knows he's said it. I don't stop and neither does he. Trystan's beautiful body is covered in sweat when he finally rolls me over and pushes up one of my legs. My jeans are gone but my panties are still on. I blink and smile. The haze grows thicker and I can't stop thinking about Sean.

Trystan watches my eyes as he slides his mouth over my body. I trail my fingers along his back, pulling him closer, wishing for things that cannot be. Trystan holds my knee tightly to my chest and rocks against me promising me things to come, of what it'll be like to have him inside of me.

I'm lost. This feels like a dream and although my fingers and my mind know this isn't Sean, I want him to be, so he is. My head feels heavy, and it's too difficult to think, but I refuse to surrender to the sleep that's pulling at me. I will not feel the water around my neck again. I want to feel flesh on flesh, the slick warmth of his body as we lie together. I can no longer tell what's real. Course fingers run over my body and passion flames within my soul. It's a dream. The way he moves is different and I can't understand why.

"Sean," I whisper. This is the way things were supposed to be, soft and sensual. Pure and perfect. His lips find that place on my neck and I gasp, digging my nails into his skin.

You're dreaming, I tell myself and get lost in the bliss. I forget that Sean and I are done. I refuse to remember what his mother said or the trade he made that ensured we were through. Even though it was my decision, I can't bear it. It feels like I'm made of glass, and brick upon brick was pressed upon me until I shattered.

There's nothing left except this heat and my nails on his hot skin. I hold onto the dream for as long as I can, following it as far as it will allow me, until a heart beats steadily beneath my ear, and we are still. The two of us stay like that, holding each other like the world is dying around us and we're the only two people left to face the remains, alone.

CHAPTER 9

The sunlight shines in my face, rousing me. Pulling up my arm, I drop it over my eyes and moan. God, my head hurts. That's when I open my eyes. Last night comes flooding back and I feel Trystan's arm draped across my naked hips. He sleeps next to me, holding me in a way I've always craved, but Sean would never tolerate.

I don't know how I feel; I'm caught between horror and denial. This didn't happen. It's not what it looks like, is it? We just embraced each other—I needed comfort and he gave it. But where did we stop? Did we stop? Clutching at my face, I sit up.

I can't remember.

The necklace with the ring is still on the floor next to Trystan, glinting in the sunlight. How many years has he worn it? Who was she and what happened to them? They're questions that I can't ask, and the answers won't make any difference. He's going to hate me for this. He's been holding a torch for this girl for God-knows-how-long and then I come along. Oh, God. I can't face him. What's he going to think? It was supposed to be a hug, an embrace, a small kiss. How did we end up like this?

Trystan's eyes open slowly when I sit up, and he tenses when his gaze drifts to my bare skin. I have the blankets pulled up to my chest, concealing the front of me. Last night comes back to him, at least in part. I see the rush of memory flood his eyes. I touch his hand, lacing our fingers together, and hold onto him tightly. "It's all right, Trystan." But my voice shakes and he can tell that I'm not all right.

"Oh God. I took advantage—" he gasps, before his jaw locks, nearly having said the wrong name, and pulls his hand back. Those sapphire eyes look away, guilt-ridden.

He finishes speaking. "Avery, I shouldn't have."

Tucking a piece of hair behind my ear, I ask, "Shouldn't have what, exactly?" I don't want to look up at him, but he's too silent for too long. The only sound I can hear is the way he breathes when he's upset, or excited. My skin is instantly covered in shivers, reacting to something that is out of reach—a memory that was never made. It slipped through my fingers like rain, but my body remembers and reacts to him.

Trystan has his head tipped down with that long dark hair covering his face. He pushes it back, and flicks his gaze up to meet mine for half a second. "I was kind of hoping you could tell me."

We stare at each other. Nothing. No one speaks. I can't remember and neither can he. I start to mutter things I shouldn't say. "If we did everything, I'd feel it, right? I've always felt it the next day with Sean, but he doesn't hold back."

His lips form a tight line, before he spits out, "Just because I didn't hurt you doesn't mean I held back, assuming things went that far." Trystan looks around, but there are only empty bottles on the floor. "Damn, my head hurts."

"I didn't mean it like that." I try to clarify, but I can't. His touch was nice, gentle. It was the difference between being fucked and making love. I haven't had much experience with the latter. I'm playing with my fingers, weaving them together and turning them, twisting them as I explain. "I meant that after I've been with Sean, I can feel it. But, I don't feel any pain and nothing's sore. So how do you normally tell?"

Trystan's eyes dart back and forth like he's remembered something. "Condoms. I always use them." We both start looking through the blankets, but there's no trace, no wrappers, nothing to indicate he used one. Trystan finds his jeans before he pulls one out that is still sealed, unused. "Fuck."

I laugh nervously. "That doesn't mean anything." He glances up at me like I'm stupid. "What? Just because we didn't use one, it doesn't mean we did it. I mean, maybe we just made out and fell asleep."

"Naked?" He's ready to roll his eyes, but doesn't. "Avery, Occam's Razor—the simplest explanation is usually the correct one. In this case, we slept together. Please tell me you're on the pill or something." He watches me, with regret pressing heavily on his shoulders.

I nod. "I am, but Trystan, there's no way to know if we did." He stands there, half-dressed, staring at me. "So let's act like we didn't."

"I don't forget lovers like that. Sex means something to me. You do something to me." He rubs his hand over his face and doesn't look at me while he says the rest. "It's like you're a lightning rod—you evoke every memory of someone I want to forget. I would have never gone after you because, even though I like you, I'd always think of her. Pathetic, isn't it?" He laughs bitterly and shakes his head. When he finally glances at me, he adds, "And don't worry, I won't tell anyone anything."

I pull my blanket higher and try not to smile. "A chivalrous rock star? Isn't that interesting?"

"Don't tease, not about this." The look on his face is barren. I can't read what he's thinking at all. I don't know if he feels like he betrayed his lost love or me.

"Trystan, I'm not. I needed to be held and comforted. I think you did, too. That's all it was, right? You shouldn't feel guilty. I kissed you, remember?" I touch his leg and he looks down at me before he sits next to me on the blankets. He gazes into my eyes with too much sorrow for one person to bear. "We're friends, aren't we?" I don't mean to sound needy, but the hitch in my voice tells everything.

"Of course." There's not an ounce of hesitation once he realizes I care about him. I've lost everything and I'm being forced to start over in a life that's been hellish for too long. He wraps his arms around me and kisses me on the cheek. "It was just this one time. An alignment of the stars."

"Always the poet." He smiles shyly, but still looks guilty. "Trystan, I'm not ready for another relationship. Go put your necklace back on and no one will know."

He nods. After a moment he says, "Just don't tell Mel. I think she has a thing for me and I'm pretty sure she's castrated a man for lesser things." He shudders and smiles.

"Plus, your boss is scary as hell and your ex, well, let's just say they'll all kill me." He looks at the ring in his palm before putting the chain back on.

Smiling, I assure him, "I won't tell anyone." Trystan holds my gaze for a moment before looking away. "And thank you. Last night was rough. Spending it with you, for the parts I remember, helped." He blushes and tries to hide it behind his hair.

"Any time." I put my hand on his shoulder and he looks down at it and then back up at me.

We stay like that for a second, until the uncertain moment passes. Suddenly, he's the man he was yesterday, before last night happened. "So, tomorrow's here. It's time to face the day, your insane boss, an assassin, and your sadistic ex. What do you have in mind, because I know there's no way in hell you're going to wait for Sean to tell you what to do?"

A grin slowly spreads across my face. "You know me so well."

CHAPTER 10

After I tell him what I want to do, Trystan protests. "There's no way you should do that, Avery. Let me go."

"Yeah, the rock star should just show up at Henry Thomas's house and ask if he's been trying to shoot me. Good plan." I roll my eyes.

"Avery, dear, I mean this in the kindest way possible, but how are you still alive?" Trystan is dressed with a faded t-shirt and a worn flannel shirt on top, coupled with a pair of ripped jeans and his Chucks. I have to admit that he's easy on the eyes. He leans back against the chair and winces. We're sitting in his old kitchen. There's dust everywhere.

"What?"

"You zealously used your nails on my back. It looks like I was mauled by a bear." My face flames red and I lunge at him to slap him. Trystan laughs. "Holy shit! You blush? You're a call girl, how are you still blushing when a guy mentions sex?"

We've been sitting at this little table in the horrible home he grew up in. It's horrible because I know this place is haunted for him, but he won't let us leave until the plan is revised. I swipe at him and miss. Trystan pulls his arm away, chuckling, "Easy there, Call Girl. I have enough marks on me to remember you by."

"Jerk."

"Don't do it if you can't talk about it later."

"So says the man who may or may not have slept with me last night." I roll my eyes. Again.

"No, I definitely slept with you. I remember pressing your knee into your chest at one point, but you were still dressed, sort of." He smiles wolfishly and I know he's teasing me, trying to see how red I can turn. "I'm not sure when the clothes came off or what you did with my boxers. They're MIA."

My jaw drops! "You're going commando?"

"Not by choice, Call Girl. For all I know you ate them." He laughs and I lunge at him again. This time I knock his elbow and he tips back in his chair. The motion almost knocks him over, but he rights himself at the last second.

"Nice move, Catwoman."

"You know I like pussy."

I make a face at him. "You did not just say that. That's something that Jon would say, not you."

"Why? Because it lacked eloquence? All men want it, Avery. You should know that by now. Love songs, at their core, are only interested in getting into your core." He's still smiling widely and I can't tell if he's serious or teasing me.

I blink twice. "Where's the Trystan I know, because this version is a little too honest for me."

"Honesty is what makes a person. At the end of his life it's one of the things people remember. Your legacy isn't left by fame or fortune. It's left by the footprints of compassion and honesty." He has no idea how astute he is, or how alluring his words are—they're so profoundly simple, modest, and perfect. No wonder why everyone loves him. Well, everyone except Sean.

"There he is, the real Trystan Scott. Okay, now that I have the normal version of you back, tell me what we should do or I'm out the door."

His dark brows furrow as his lips press together. Finally, he mutters, "You're so stubborn."

"The word you're looking for is stupid." I bat my eyelashes at him and toss my hair over my shoulder for emphasis. Trystan doesn't react. He sits there with a stern, Sean-like disapproving expression. "I can't hide forever."

"You shouldn't have to, but wait for Sean to find out. You said he'd know shortly." Trystan tips back in his chair and folds his hands behind his head. "Let him do it."

"You don't know what he traded."

Trystan leans forward and the chair goes with him, the first two legs slamming down on the floor. "I have an idea, but I don't really understand why you care. You left him, didn't you?"

"I…" I didn't want to. I wanted him to come after me, to chase me, and convince me that we belong together, but he didn't. Instead, Sean promised he was leaving and I wasn't going with him. He'll return to his fake fiancée in California and I'll stay here and be Miss Black's pawn for whatever the hell she wants on Long Island. "…don't want to talk about it."

He puts his hands up, palms toward me. "Fine by me."

"So, then let's go."

"All right, but I'm coming with you."

I sigh as I pick up my purse and make my way to the door. "Trystan we've already been over this. I have to talk to him alone."

"Yeah, not happening."

I turn and wave a finger in his face. "Don't make me call Gabe."

"Gabe is already outside if the guy is any good at his job." Trystan sighs and finally caves. "Fine, but you only have five minutes. Then I'm coming in."

"I can take care of myself." I think about the pilot and a cold feeling grips my chest. It freezes me to the core and makes me feel sick. The scene replays in my head until there is blood spilling across the floor, creeping toward me like the monster I've become.

"I believe you." His voice drops like he knows I've done something I shouldn't have. He watches too closely, and sees too much. It makes me uncomfortable.

I turn quickly so those knowing eyes can't read mine. "Great, then let's go."

———

The deal had been for Trystan to drive me to Henry's and then wait in the car, but along the way, we stop and pick up a guy who looks like he ate a pickup truck. Trystan's bodyguard is all muscle. He doesn't speak or look at me. He just sits there, way too big for the space in the back of Trystan's limo, with his dark arms folded over his massive chest. Each bicep is the size of a bowling ball. Damn, the man is huge.

He glances at me with a look that could kill. Black eyes narrow in on me and when he finally speaks, his voice is way deeper than I'd thought. "This is idiotic."

"Wow, do you always talk to Trystan's friends that way?" Okay, that sounded bitchy, even to me.

It doesn't faze him. "I only speak to Trystan's friends that way. You should have listened to Ferro."

I glance at Trystan and give him a death look. "You told him?"

Trystan is slumped back into the seat across from me. It showcases his age. I forget that Sean is older. Trystan has a lazy confidence that speaks volumes. It says he's doing what he thinks is best and that I'm a moron.

Jabbing his thumb at the bodyguard, Trystan explains, "I had to tell him. As it is, he wanted to kill me for disappearing last night and not telling them. If I get shot, they don't get paid. It's the ultimate job failure when you're in his profession. Hence, the irritation at your impending idiocy." Trystan offers a crooked grin.

I want to punch him. "So what would you do, Muscle Man? Crack Henry Thomas like a crab leg and toss him into the bay?"

"That's one way to find out, however subtlety is more desirable in this situation. What if my boy is seen with you and caught up in this mess? Did you think of him at all before you dragged him into this with you?" Holy shit, he's scolding me? Trystan sits there, bright blue eyes sparkling, trying not to laugh. My mouth opens to defend myself, but the guy doesn't stop. "And another thing, what the fuck do you think is going to happen here? You really think you can march up to this guy's front door and he'll just tell you that he's been trying to put a bullet in your head? Things don't work that way princess, wake up."

I blink at him. "Are you done?"

"No." But the man doesn't add anything else.

When he doesn't speak, I say, "I'll be able to tell."

"Uh-uh." The big man looks out the window, not even asking me to elaborate.

"I know this guy."

"Yeah, as if your gut instinct is perfect." The guy practically growls at me.

My eyes flick to Trystan. "What's he talking about?"

"Miss Black," Trystan replies.

"You told him that too!"

"No, he already knew." Trystan and I look at the bodyguard with questions in our eyes. "I like how no one calls her by her first name."

The big man visibly shivers and works his jaw before he can manage to spit some words out. "It's because her first name is Satan. Do you know how many men I've worked with that have been lured away by her? Let's just say that I've heard stories and no amount of money could make me consider working for her."

I'm not sure if he's talking about being a bodyguard or not. The guy is majorly creeped out and I'm not sure why. "You wouldn't be a bodyguard for one of her girls?"

The man looks over at me and laughs. He shakes his bald head and then looks at Trystan, and then back to me. "You have no idea what kind of shit you've stepped in, do you? You think she's just a madam? If you don't learn to read between the lines, she'll kill you—never mind this idiot who missed."

My skin covers in bumps as a chill washes over me. When I don't speak, Trystan asks, "What else does she do?"

But the bodyguard shakes his head. "The less you know, the better. Just stay the fuck away from Black and her girls."

"So, stashing one of Black's girls who might be wanted for murder is probably bad then, huh?" Trystan gives the guy a half smile.

"Shit, Scott. Tell me you didn't have anything to do with it." The big man seems like he's ready to pounce on Trystan. His eyes are flamethrowers and his words are short and threatening.

"I didn't kill the hooker at the hotel, and I wasn't at the hotel, but I was at the strip club when this girl and her friend wandered in after the fact. Bob, don't act like that. It's nothing, and Mel didn't do it anyway. All of this sounds like a set up to get at Avery."

I can't help it, I giggle. "Bob! Your name is Bob?"

The muscle man turns on me and the laughter runs and hides. The smile runs from my lips and falls to the bottom of the bay. Bob doesn't respond. He looks out the window, thinking, until we pull up a block from the Thomas house.

The car stops and Trystan shakes his head. "Don't do this."

"I have to. I can't have things this way. Sean can't owe his mother a thing because of me."

Trystan smiles and sighs. "I knew it was about him. This direct approach, it's so you can cut off his mother's attempt to find out and he won't owe her anything. Damn it, Avery. Sean's a grown man. If Ferro wants to leave, let him. You can't hold onto someone who doesn't want to be held. Believe me, I know."

I'm lost in his eyes for a moment, seeing one of his long banished memories dance before me exposed and vulnerable. I touch the back of his hand, lightly. "One life touches another and changes it forever…for better or worse. We don't know unless we try, right?"

The corners of his mouth tip up. "A life without love is not a life at all. Is that what you're saying to the man who had his heart torn from his chest?"

"We're all the same. Have you realized that? Me, you, Jon the jerk, Bryan, and Sean. Peter seems normal." I make a face.

Trystan laughs. "The man swing dances. Plus, he has Sydney. He's happy and that's the antithesis of normal." We both laugh before Trystan takes a long slow pull of air through his open mouth. "I'll kill him if he hurts you." He's dead serious.

"I know."

We stare at each other, but no one speaks. I have no idea what's between us. All I can notice is how much he seems like Sean sometimes. It's like Trystan is a mirror of Sean's past. I suppose that's what Trystan sees when he looks at me. The girl who got away, the woman whose name didn't quite slip past those pink lips last night. I feel bad for him. Hell, I feel bad for me. We're both love-struck and the person we hold dearest is gone. I get the feeling Trystan told her to take a walk the same way I told Sean I couldn't do this anymore.

I want tender touches. I need hugs. I can't go on with the constant roughness and head games.

I'm not sure who could.

I touch Trystan's hand, which makes him drop his gaze and look at the touch. "There's no such thing as destiny or soul mates. Luck comes to those who take it. I'm taking it. Please understand."

"Oh, I do. All too well, actually. If you're not back in five minutes, Bob is coming. If Bob doesn't come back, I'm coming, and you don't want me in there."

I smile like he's cute, until Bob shakes his head. "The boy has a temper."

"Stop calling me that." Trystan and Bob seem to have known each other for a while. I wonder if Bob was around when the papers found out the heartthrob Day Jones was actually Trystan Scott.

"Yes, sir." Bob grins at Trystan and they both laugh. Then, Bob points a sausage of a finger in my face. "Five minutes, Miss Stanz. That's it. And try to find out more information than what your gut tells you, since it seems to be misleading you at times." Bob offers a smug look before opening the door.

CHAPTER 11

I'm standing before Henry's huge house. A towering black door, with panels of glass and wrought iron nearly twenty feet high, rises before me. My heart beats faster. If he's been trying to kill me, will he be dumb enough to shoot me on his porch? I lean in and ring the bell.

I have no idea what I'm going to say, if I should be direct or do something else. I should have thought this part through more, but something told me that I couldn't come up with a plan. I'd have to play it the best I could, because I have no idea how he's going to react. On our last visit, Gabe kicked the crap out of him after he tried to beat me to death. Okay, I see Bob's point a little clearer now, but I'm not letting Mrs. Ferro have a thing to hold over Sean's head, not if I can help it.

The door opens and a man in a suit is standing there. He's older, thin, and has a white mustache with grayish skin. He looks ill. Even so, he stands with perfect posture, just like Henry. "Yes?"

"I'm here to see Mr. Thomas." Suddenly, I feel under dressed. I'm wearing jeans and Trystan's shirt with a pair of old Chucks. I straighten like I belong here and don't drop my gaze. Tucking a piece of hair behind my ear, I add, "He's expecting me."

"Come in." The man steps back and leads me into a massive foyer of marble and stone. Everything is white and cream rock. It's cold and beautiful at the same time. "I'll tell him you're here. A name, madam?"

"Avery." I look around at the artwork on the walls, the paleness of it. There's no color to be found, not here. It's almost as if he wanted to present a sterile version of himself before letting his guests into his house. I wonder if each room is different, if Henry will lead me to a rainbow room because that's what I'd like most or if the entire house is like this.

A massive staircase is to my left and a moment later I hear footfalls coming from above my head. When Henry comes into sight, I freeze. Fear pumps through my veins the way it did before. I have three minutes before Bob shows up. Talk fast. Say something.

"Henry, it's good to see you."

His eyes scan my body. "So this is what you look like during daylight hours. Creatures of the night are typically deceitful, but this transformation is remarkable. Give my compliments to your employer."

"Miss Black will be grateful to hear it."

He grins like a wolf about to devour a pack of sheep. "Not that boss, the other one. Or haven't you heard who you're really working for?" He taps his finger to his chin and cocks his head to the side. "Innocent or naïve? Those two traits walk hand in hand, and with you it's so hard to tell."

"Wow, that was flattering." My brows lift and my snark comes out. I can't help it. He's still standing four steps above me, looking down on me like I'm trash.

"I only speak the truth." His British accent comes through stronger on that phrase.

I march up the stairs so that we're on the same step. Tipping my head to the side, I ask, "Then tell me, who's been trying to shoot me?"

Henry's smile falls like a monkey from a tree. Plop. Dead on the forest floor. "What do you mean?"

"Last night, for example, where were you?"

He laughs and presses a hand to his chest. "You're a presumptive whore. How dare you question me? I offered you a life that most women could only dream about and you turned me down. You have no right to be here." He snaps his fingers and the man who let me in reappears. Henry turns on the stairs and takes a step up. "Show her out."

"I wouldn't do that." He turns and looks down at me. "There's a bodyguard due to come plowing through that door any second now. Tell me what I want to know and I'm gone."

Henry's gaze cuts to the door and then to the servant. He's seriously annoyed. "Leave us." When we're alone, Henry slides his gaze over my body again, like I'm the hooker he ordered. "You need to know who you are working for."

"And I suppose you know?"

"Of course. After Black's thug broke my ribs I wanted to make sure the correct person was repaid that kindness." He smiles viciously.

"You tried to strangle me."

"Only a little. Some girls like it." He winks at me.

"What do I have to do to get the name?"

He gives me a coy grin. "Me."

I make a disgusted sound. "Yeah, I don't think so. No freebies."

"Still hung up on Ferro?"

"No, he's gone actually and if you didn't act like such an asshole I would have gone out with you in a heartbeat. Better play your asshole card closer to your chest next time. You have less than 60 seconds by the way. Where were you last night?"

He gets in my face and beams that arrogant smile that the wealthy master in grade school. It's irritating. "With your friend, having the good time you didn't enjoy."

"I want a name. Now."

"Of course. Her name is Amber. I came by to see you, but you weren't there. She invited me into her bed and I accepted. I left when her boyfriend came."

"You admit that you were in my room last night?" I don't know what to do with this information. I expected him to deny knowing anything.

"Of course."

"It's rather convenient that the only person who can vouch for you is dead."

His snarky smile fades. "She's dead?"

I tap my forehead. "Bullet. And then someone shot the shit out of my bed assuming it was me. You're lucky you were gone or that could have been you."

His skin pales to paper white and he sits down hard. Henry's gaze becomes unfocused as he stares across the room. "The boy was shot, too?"

"Yes. A lot."

He looks up at me. "We had sex in your bed. I wanted you, so we—" He closes his eyes and pinches his temples.

"Who else saw you?" When he doesn't answer, I tap him with my foot. I can see Bob out the window, headed toward the door. "I need a name. Now!"

Bob pounds on the front door, which snaps Henry back to life. "The girl with the long black hair, a few doors down. She was asking Amber about her roommate."

"Asia?"

He nods just as the door flies open. Bob punched it. The two slabs of glass splinter and go flying across the marble floor as the doors burst open. Henry looks over at Bob as I skip down the steps. "Come on. I got what we need." I turn to look at Henry. "If you come near me, Bob will snap you like a lightstick and hang your body on a tree in Heckscher. Got it?" Henry nods.

CHAPTER 12

"I need a phone!" Trystan won't give me mine.

He shakes his head. "Sean said if he can find you, we screwed up. No phone."

"Asia saw him last night. She can say what time and confirm Henry's story."

"And if she does? Then what?"

"Then it's not him and we start over." I look out the car window. We've been driving in circles because he doesn't want to go back to his dad's house.

Trystan's phone rings. He answers it. "Ferro." He looks over at me. "Yeah, she's fine. No, I haven't let her do anything stupid, unless I count."

I slap him hard as my eyes go wide. "Don't say that!"

Trystan covers the phone with his hand. "He won't believe me anyway." Trystan returns to his call. "And what the hell am I supposed to do with her tonight? I'm playing at the Garden. It's not like I can cancel a show." He's quiet, and then adds. "Don't think you're the only one who cares about her, dipshit. If I didn't, I wouldn't have taken her with me. So find out what you need to know before it's too fucking late." He hangs up. Wrinkles line his normally smooth face before he throws his phone at the seat across from us. It bounces off and hits Bob. Trystan grabs his face in his hands and sighs.

I plead. "Let me talk to Asia, then. Let's drive by."

"I can't let you go inside."

"What if everyone came outside?" I raise a brow, coming up with a crazy idea. When I tell Trystan the idea, to my surprise, he agrees.

———

When we enter the quad at my college, Trystan and I split up, but not too far. He stays out in the open and sits under a tree with a guitar on his lap. I walk by a group of girls and press Trystan's phone to my ear. It's not on, but it looks like I'm talking to someone. "I swear to God, it's Trystan Scott. He's under a tree in the quad. Get over here!" They hear me and start squealing. I walk in a circle and repeat the same thing a few times in front of different groups of people. Instantly, students and teachers start to come out of the surrounding buildings and flock to him.

I wait outside my building. Asia will come out. I know she will. It seems like she's the last person to find out, but when she does, the girl comes racing down the stairs and flies out the door. Halfway across the quad, I fall into step with her. We're in a mass of people. "Hey, Asia!"

"Avery!" She stops, hugs me, and sounds giddy. "Is it really him?" She looks across the quad, standing on her tippie toes, trying to see past all the people.

"Yeah, it is. He's singing. It's the coolest thing ever." We walk together and talk about Trystan. She's really excited, so I get straight to it. "Was there a guy in Amber's room last night, before Naked Guy?"

Her lip curls. "Yeah, the old British dude. He was such a prick. He slammed the door on me when he was leaving. Where is the whore, anyway? She skipped finals today and even though she's a total Skankerella, it was unlike her."

They don't know? How is that possible? Lying, I say, "I'm not sure. Have fun listening to Trystan play. I'll be right back."

"You're not staying?"

"I need to grab something from my room." Well, I actually need to see if my dead roommate is still there. How could the entire night pass and nobody noticed?

Even though I promised Trystan and Sean that I wouldn't go into the dorm again, I do. I run up the stairs and down the empty halls until I get to my room. The silence is a little eerie. My skin prickles as those horrible memories of Amber with blood dripping down her face reappear vividly in my mind. It's my fault she's dead. I even feel bad for Naked Guy. He was a jackass, but Mel pounding him was enough for me. I didn't need him killed, not like that. As I think about it my stomach twists. He was shot several times, in places that don't kill, tortured until the final shot went through his head.

Stop! By the time I reach my room, I'm scolding myself to stop. I'm so nervous that I'm shaking and my body is ready to wretch. The silence just makes it worse. Everyone must have run out to see Trystan.

As I reach for my knob, key in hand, I tremble. I don't want to see that bloody scene again. It was so horrific, but I unlock the door and push it open. After I scan the room, my jaw drops.

She's gone.

He's gone.

There's no blood, no trace of anything. I stagger back and shiver, wrapping my arms tightly around my middle. Where are the bodies? How'd the blood come out of the white bedspread? There isn't a drop. There's no trace that anything happened here last night at all.

I glance at my dresser and grab my Mom's cross and stuff it into my pocket. I'm so scared, so terrified. Only someone with money and power could clean this up without anyone noticing, and only two people come to mind—Black and Mrs. Ferro. For a second, I'm afraid it was Sean. Even whore-y Amber deserves a funeral. Her family will never know what happened to her. It'll look like she ran off with Naked Guy right before graduation. No one will know they were murdered right here in this room.

The hairs on the back of my neck prickle as I feel eyes on my back. I round swiftly and scream, ready to throw a punch.

"Hey, calm down little miss ninja." Marty has his hands up, palms facing me. "What's wrong, skittish chick? I've been looking for you, and from the looks of it, you're in serious need of an ice cream binge." He leans on the doorframe, and folds his arms across his chest. His sandy hair is slicked back, and today he's wearing a suit that makes him look like one of the dudes on Mad Men.

When I realize it's him, I slap his arm and squeak, "Don't sneak up on me like that!"

Marty laughs. "I wasn't exactly quiet."

"You know what I mean." My voice quivers when I speak, even though I try to hide it. Marty straightens and looks down at me with concern, but I don't offer any hints as to what's bothering me. It's bad enough that I pulled Trystan into this. I'm not risking Marty, too. I have to get out of here. I race around my room and grab the few relics that matter most to me, besides the cross. There are only a handful of objects. I stuff them in my book bag after dumping out the educational contents on the floor and kicking them into my closet.

When I open the door, I half expect to see ashen Amber sitting there with her ghostly pale lips parted in an eternal cry for help, but she's gone. The clothes and contents are exactly as I left them.

Marty follows me around the room like a puppy, yipping questions, "Where've you been? I thought you went to work with Black and didn't bother to say good-bye. Avery," he grabs my left hand and looks down at my bare fingers. "Oh my God, you broke it off with him?" He holds my hand and stares at the bare finger that once held a beautiful engagement ring.

I yank my palm back. "Yeah, and I don't feel like talking about it."

"So you're taking the job with Black?"

"I don't know! Stop asking me questions I can't answer! Stop acting like you're my goddamn brother, because you're not! I don't need you looking out for me. I don't need your sympathy or your ice cream. Just give me some space, okay? Is that too much to ask? The past few weeks have been Hell and I need some room to breathe." It's over the top, but I need him mad at me. Leave already. I can't drag him into this.

He laughs. "You think I'm smothering you? That's hysterical. If you think this is closeness, no wonder why you don't have a ring on your finger anymore."

My gaze narrows to a slit as I step toward him and push the massive man in the chest with my fingertips. This time the anger is real. "Don't you dare judge me! You're the one who said to do whatever it takes. You're the one who said sell pot to freshmen, that hooking was only for a little while, to take the next job with Black, or did you forget, you fucking asshole?" Marty's brow raises and he still has an amused smile on his face. I shove him again. "Stop laughing at me! Do you think this is funny? Do you think I'm enjoying this? Well, I'm not! I don't want to be here anymore and I don't want to see you, so leave me alone." I shove past him and head toward the door.

"Avery, come on. I didn't mean it like that."

"Yes, you did. You enjoy judging people. Meanwhile, you lie as good as the rest of them, or did you forget gay boy?" His lips part like I punched him in the stomach. "Yeah, I thought so. There's nothing more to say here."

I'm down the hall and in the stairwell by the time I hear his voice again. "So who are you banging tonight? Maybe I should just put in another order with your boss!" I give him the finger and don't look back.

As I cross the quad toward Trystan, he nods, acknowledging that he sees me before I veer left. The car is waiting. I slip inside and start to cry. By the time Trystan jumps in—the man has to literally launch himself through the door to escape the grabby hands of his fans—I've wiped most of the sorrow away, but the stains still linger, glistening on my cheeks.

He doesn't say anything. Instead, Trystan sits next to me and holds out his arms. I let him hold me the way I wish that Sean would. I lean against his soft flannel and inhale his scent, comparing it to Sean's. They're nothing alike. Trystan keeps his arm around me until we arrive at Madison Square Garden.

When the car stops, he says, "I have to go and get ready for the show later. I want you to come with me, and stay by me."

"How am I supposed to do that?" If I stand in the darkness of the stage wings while he sings, he can't see me. There's no way I'm going to get closer to him than that.

Trystan grins. "Wait and see."

CHAPTER 13

I'm on stage during the rehearsal and sound check, sitting on a stool. When Trystan disappears backstage to change, he takes me with him. After he strips his shirt, he teases, "No looking."

It makes me smile. I turn around and wander through the dressing room. "So where am I supposed to stand while you rock out and make women orgasm as they watch you sing?"

"Wow, I never thought of that." He sounds intrigued.

"Trystan," I scold.

"I usually think they have a crush, but you made it sound dirty." He presses a button and tells someone they can come in.

A crew of make-up and hair people surround him. It must suck to have so many people touching him like that all at once. It's like he's not human. They tug, touch, and brush as if he were a doll. Trystan just sits there silently until they leave. When he turns back to me, I can't help it.

I laugh. "Nice eyeliner. It's darker than mine."

"Bite me."

"It's okay, I know it's part of the show."

"I feel like my whole life is a show. I'm a fucking fraud." I don't know what he means, but the somber look snaps and he's back to his smiley self. "So, now we need your costume."

My brows furrow. "Rock star say what?"

He retrieves a piece of cloth that was laid out on a chair, along with stockings. "Put this on. There are heels in the closet and wigs. Choose one and someone will come and finish your make-up. You'll have more eyeliner than I do, by the way."

I stare at the mesh outfit in my hand. It's a body suit that's almost sheer. "Are you kidding me?"

"It's what all the dancers wear. One of them usually dances with me, well, more like licks my chest and slides against me during the show. Tonight, you're taking her spot. Just wear that and stand by me. No one will think it's you." I hesitate. Trystan comes toward me, still barefoot. He has no shirt on and they've made his abs look more ripped than they already are with stage make-up and an airbrushing machine. "I won't let him get to you. If you're next to me, he can't take a shot at you, even if the guy knows who you are. It's a public place. Getting a gun in here is nearly impossible and I'll know you're safe. And if you don't want to lick me, you don't have to." He's trying not to smile when he says the last part.

I laugh and shove him aside. "Fine, where do I change?"

"Are you kidding?" I stare at him and shake my head. "You can't leave my sight. You're changing in here, and it's not just because I like seeing you naked." He winks, which makes me roll my eyes.

I reply, "I could have liked you if you didn't say that last part."

"Yeah," he laughs, "And, I could have liked you if you didn't drive me crazy." He stares at me for a moment and I swear he's seeing someone else. I break the stare and throw my arms around his neck and peck his cheek.

"Thank you."

"For what?" He looks confused.

"For what? For looking out for me. For following me around. For making sure I'm safe. You act like it's nothing, like you'd do it for anyone."

"No, you're not just anyone." His gaze drops to the floor. "Go change over there. I'll keep my eyes to myself."

CHAPTER 14

After I have on the costume, which consists of stocking like material with blacked out fishnet over tiny areas of my boobs and crotch, I grab a blonde wig and a pair of heels. I feel ridiculous wearing this thing. When I step toward Trystan, he turns around. The man's jaw drops and I swear it's ten minutes before he remembers to blink. "Wow."

"You've seen me naked and now you say wow."

"Yes, look at yourself." He steps aside from the mirror and when I don't walk toward it, he takes my shoulders and shoves me. Gripping my arms, he whispers in my ear, "You have no idea how beautiful you are, do you?"

His question makes me squirm. I laugh nervously. "I'm not a cover model."

"No," my stomach dips when he confesses it, but he continues, "You're more beautiful, by far."

"Trystan." I try to twist out of his grip, but he holds onto me.

"Look at yourself Avery. Why can't you see what the rest of us already know? You're stunning."

"I'm too heavy."

He laughs. "You're real. Every curve is perfect, from your lips to your ass. Seriously. Accept it. If you don't, some asshole will take advantage of you." There's a knock at the door. "Speak of the devil."

When the door opens, my heart stops. "Sean."

His eyes go wide and darken as his gaze moves slowly over my costume. He speaks to Trystan without looking at him. "Scott."

"Asshole."

"I should break your pretty face for letting her approach Thomas today."

I reach out and take Sean's hand. "I did that."

"Yes," Sean smiles at me. "I know. But I told your friend here to keep you safe, and walking into that lunatic's home alone was foolish. The fact that he let you tells me how big of an idiot he truly is."

"Sean, Henry didn't do it. And the bodies, they're gone." This confession leaves both men shocked into silence.

They say in unison, "How do you know?"

I shrink back a little bit, waiting for the onslaught of screaming. "I went into my room after I talked to Asia. She said that she saw Henry leave and seemed to have no clue that Amber and Naked Guy were dead. She was happy, and there was no yellow tape or cops. So I opened the door. Everything was spotless, exactly the way it'd been before they were shot."

"Holy shit." Trystan stares at me and then locks his jaw to keep from saying more.

Sean has a blank expression on his face. I wish he'd react so I can tell he still cares about me. "Scott, get me an all areas pass.

I'm staying near her tonight. We're missing something."

Trystan nods and then walks over to a couch and sits down, leaving me standing in front of Sean. My ex-fiancée's face is devoid of any readable expression. He's made of stone once more and I doubt I'll ever see the softer side of him again.

I ask, "Did your mother tell you the same thing?"

"She hasn't said, yet. Knowing her, she won't tell me anything until she knows everything."

"Well, tell her to stop. I don't want you owing her."

Sean just breathes. He's so close, but it feels like he's miles away. I've been longing for him, wishing for things that will never be. He's too damaged, too far gone. The monster within has taken over and I'll never see inside his soul again. That last ember was snuffed out and the worst part is that I'm the one who did it when I gave him back my ring.

My eyes catch a lump under his shirt and then rise to the chain around his neck. I go to reach for it, but Sean's hand juts out and stops me. "Don't." It's one word but it means so much.

Don't expose the ring.

Don't make me say I still want you.

Don't put us through that again.

Just don't.

CHAPTER 15

Sean stays with me, and Trystan won't let me out of his sight. We go to the stage before they let the crowd in and Trystan shows me where to stand. "Shake your ass and you'll blend in fine."

When I looked in the mirror, after they were done with my make-up and hair, my own mother wouldn't recognize me. Long blonde hair trails down my back and there are other dancers milling about who look identical. Some have blonde hair, some have red. There's not a brunette in sight, which makes me wonder if that's Trystan's type since it's so glaringly absent, and because I look like her, the woman with no name.

Sean doesn't comment, he only watches until Trystan retreats to below the stage. The pre-show band is setting up. I'm supposed to stay with Sean in the wing until Trystan is on stage. I shiver and rub my hands over my arms.

Sean's gaze flicks to the side, noticing. He silently moves behind me and asks, "Are you cold?" I shake my head. I can't speak due to the massive lump in my throat. I may not see him after tonight. If Mrs. Ferro finds the killer before we do, she'll take care of it, and then he'll be gone.

It's as if he knows what I'm thinking. Sean steps toward me and rubs his hands over my bare arms. "He won't be able to get you here."

"Sean, he's tried over and over again, and each time was at night. I'm scared." My voice is faint, barely audible above the noise.

"No one will hurt you here. There are too many guards. When Scott first told me this idea, I thought he was insane. But it's the safest place for you tonight. Security is everywhere, plus I'm here. Nothing can hurt you, not tonight."

For a second, I think he's going to ask me about last night, about what happened between Trystan and me. Instead, he says, "I know you like him." Sean's voice is so tense that I can't stand it, but he continues to rub the goose bumps off of my arms by sliding his strong hands over my skin.

I stare straight ahead. I want to say, *He's not you*, but that won't change anything—so I remain silent.

"It's all right, Avery. I'd rather see you with him than Black."

Looking straight ahead, I confess, "Trystan doesn't care for me like that."

Sean laughs and pulls me closer, pressing his chest to my back. "Then why do I hate him so much? And don't tell me he hasn't kissed you again or done more. I'm not blind, Avery. He's what you want me to be, I see that."

My stomach twists and drops when he implies that he knows we were together. He can't know. Even I'm not certain about how far things went last night, but it doesn't keep my face from heating up. For once, I'm glad I'm facing away from him. "You hate everyone."

"No, not everyone." His breath slides across my ear, warm and welcome. God, I miss this.

"I know. I feel that ring I gave you pressing against my back." It's so chunky that holding me tight makes it obvious that it's the ring I gave him when I intended to propose. Sean's reaction is to release me, but I grab hold of his hands.

"Don't." I echo the phrase he'd spoken moments ago.

CHAPTER 16

Sean holds me like that, his arms around my waist, pressed against my back, until the preshow is over and the crowd is pumped for Trystan. Something inside me speaks loudly, telling me to savor these moments, because they'll never come again. I thought I'd lost Sean once, but it didn't feel like this. A premonition races through my body over and over again of loss and pain—crippling grief, yet to come, trying to grab hold of my throat and choke me, but I chase it away. It's just nerves.

The crowd is screaming wildly as the lights go out and smoke fills the stage. Strobes start to flash as the intro to Trystan's latest song begins. It's not the sweet love song he was known for when he began his career. His music has turned dark and edgy, and sharp as a knife. The lyrics are jarring and raw, just the way his fans like them.

Trystan's voice resonates as his half naked body emerges from the smoke. He sings:

"It's my life and
I'll lie before they make me.
It's my heart
and I'll die before she takes it.
There's no going back,
no yesterday, no tomorrow.
There's only right now,
and baby, I'll take away your sorrow."

God, he's so not over her. As the thought crosses my mind, my eyes look for her ring, but there's a huge cross around his neck. The ring isn't there, and come to think of it, I've never seen a picture of him wearing it. He keeps that part of his past a secret. I suppose I could have Googled him and looked up who he was with when he was discovered, but that's his life and nothing about it is private. I want him to tell me about her when he's ready and right now he isn't—that day may never come. I realize it, but I still hope he'll tell me, that he trusts me the way I trust him.

My feelings for Trystan are skewed. He's a young Sean to me, a shadow of the man who has his arms around my waist.

Why do I pick such damaged friends?

Like calls to like, soul calls to soul, echoes in my mind despite the deafening music.

I don't want to leave Sean's side. The pit of my stomach drops like it's the last time he'll hold me and I can't help but feel like it's an omen. I don't belong here. The killer is in the crowd. I don't know how I know, but I know. I try to tell Sean, but it's too late. They're already pushing me onto the stage with the other dancers.

I head for Trystan and pretend he's Sean, young and scared. The man sings his heart out, holding back nothing. No wonder his fans love him so much. I dance provocatively around him until he grabs me, pulling me toward him so our hips mash together. He tips me back and I bend so that my hair dangles on the floor as the band blares behind us. I see Sean in the wing, watching.

When Trystan pulls me up, his blue eyes burn with passion. He means every word he sings and I finally realize how much of a release this is for him, to be on stage like this and bearing his soul. It's his catharsis. His eyebrows flick up when we enter the part of the song where I'm supposed to slide down the front of his body and slip my tongue over his abs. The other dancers would die to be in my spot, but I can't do something so meaningful as if it were nothing.

Trystan smiles at me, like he knows. He changes the act and grabs my wrist, spinning me around and holding me in front of him, locking our bodies together tightly. I face the audience, but I can't look out at the crowd. Jealous women in front of the stage scream insults while others just scream hysterically. Trystan begins singing again, forcing my head to tip to the side. He licks my neck between breaths. The sensation startles me. I spin around, ready to slap him, but he stops me and pushes me away. The crowd eats it up and screams louder. The song is about how he doesn't need me—or her. For a moment, I'm the girl he's singing about and he tosses me away. It's what the girls in the crowd want, because a hurt, unloved Trystan in need of attention, is so much more appealing than a happy married man.

Everyone can see how broken he is, Trystan doesn't try to hide it. It spills over his lips and rolls off his tongue. He's the polar opposite of Sean in that regard.

I continue to dance around him, approaching and then being rebuffed by the rock star. We're close to the edge of the stage when I stop and place my hands on my hips. I plan on giving Trystan a death stare when something catches my eye. There are a million things glinting and glowing, so I don't know why I look to that spot, but I do.

Marty stares back at me and ice licks my spine and fills my stomach with dread. Everyone around him is moving—dancing and screaming—but his stillness is wrong. Something is going to happen. Marty's eyes lock on mine, before drifting to the wing where Sean stands.

I was wrong.

No, no, no! I glance over at Sean and look wide-eyed at him as fear floods through me. They weren't trying to kill me all this time, someone was gunning for Sean, and the killer is standing in the audience unnaturally calm with his hand in his suit pocket and his hair slicked back the way it was earlier today.

The world stops as the realization slams into place. The pilot, Amber, the hookers, and Naked Guy—they were all attempts to kill Sean. I got in the way and the man who orchestrated it is standing in the crowd with his features filled with jealousy and rage.

Four things occur simultaneously—I turn to run off stage and warn Sean, a shot is fired, and Sean runs at me, knocking me to the ground. Even though screaming ensues all around me, the world blurs and I'm deafened to the chaos.

The first sound I hear is my voice and the ear-piercing scream coming from my throat. Sean is on top of me, his massive body shielding mine. Trystan is fighting his bodyguards to get to me as they pull him away. He's swearing like he'll kill each of them for dragging him out of there, but they do. Another set of guards surround us as the houselights come on. People are running, trampling each other, trying to get out of the stadium, but I don't look at them. I whimper and wonder why Sean hasn't moved or spoken. He should have carried me away by now, but he's not moved an inch since he knocked me to the stage floor.

My hands must be gripping him so tightly, but I can't stop. The guards pry my fingers off of Sean and there's a medic asking me questions that I don't answer. I can't. He speaks to someone I can't see and they confirm shots were fired. That's when I notice how wet my stomach feels. Warmth spills around me and I finally notice we're laying in a pool of blood. Sean's eyes are locked on mine and blink slowly.

I whisper his name, as terror takes hold of me. When they finally rip us apart, we're both covered in blood. It's everywhere, but I don't feel any pain. I wonder if I've been shot, and run my hands over my bodysuit, but nothing feels wrong. A medic insists that I stay still until they rip the center of the suit off of me and wash away the blood.

Then the medic next to me, the one working on Sean, says into his transmitter, "We need the bus now! Move it to the back of the Garden. Gunshot victim. Thirty year old male, six foot, a buck seventy-five. Multiple bullet wounds to the side. He's bleeding out."

I shove past them and get to Sean's head before they can stop me. He looks into my eyes and smiles. It's so wrong, so peaceful, that I can't hold back the sob that bubbles up my throat. "Don't leave me. Sean! Please, please don't leave me!"

He parts his lips to speak, but I can't understand. His eyes flicker closed and the world is shattered with a scream that rips from my body.

THE ARRANGEMENT VOL 16

To ensure you don't miss the next installment, text AWESOMEBOOKS (one word) to 22828 and you will get an email reminder on release day.

*****

THE FERRO BROTHER MOVIE

Vote now to make it happen!
http://www.ipetitions.com/petition/ferro/

*****

This is a fan driven series. When fans ask for more, there's more.

Go to Facebook and join the discussion!

*****

COMING SOON

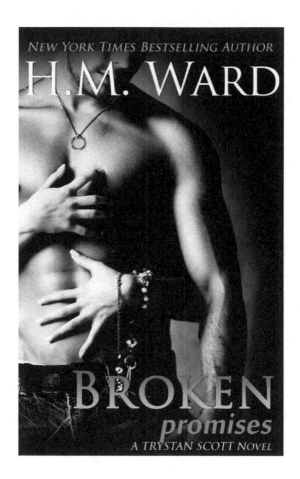

BROKEN PROMISES

A Trystan Scott Novel

READ MORE ABOUT CHARACTERS IN THIS BOOK:

BRYAN FERRO

~THE PROPOSITION~

*****

SEAN FERRO

~THE ARRANGEMENT~

******

PETER FERRO GRANZ

~DAMAGED~

******

JONATHAN FERRO

~STRIPPED~

******

TRYSTAN SCOTT

~COLLIDE~

MORE ROMANCE BOOKS BY H.M. WARD:

DAMAGED

DAMAGED 2

STRIPPED

SCANDALOUS

SCANDALOUS 2

SECRETS

THE SECRET LIFE OF
TRYSTAN SCOTT

And more.

To see a full book list, please visit:

www.SexyAwesomeBooks.com/books.htm

CAN'T WAIT FOR H.M WARD'S NEXT STEAMY BOOK?

Let her know by leaving stars and
telling her what you liked about

THE ARRANGEMENT VOL. 15

in a review!